First printing, 2024
leightonharbuck@gmail.com
www.leightonharbuck.arcrealty.com

Dedicated to Cortnee Alexander Gilchrist, my childhood best friend. I remember the day we told each other 'goodbye' so clearly and the emotions that came with me moving away. So thankful, that after many years that passed us by, we still have stayed true friends throughout all of the seasons of our lives.

Palmer, Payton, and Tripp: I hope one day you have a friendship like your mom and I do. It is the best blessing.
I love you all!

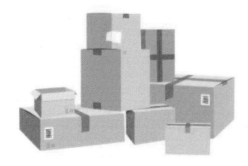

FROM A HOUSE
TO A HOME

WRITTEN BY:
LEIGHTON HARBUCK

One summer morning,
on a bright and sunny day,
my parents told me
that we were moving away.

My heart just sank
as the news was shared with me,
I wanted to say NO!
and run away as fast as I could flee!

How could I leave my home,
that was all I ever knew?
Leaving my room, my school, my friends,
was something I just could not do!

My parents tried to cheer me up and
shared that moving could be fun!
So with a brave, but uneasy heart,
I told them it could be done!

I was sad to say goodbye to friends,
and leave them all behind,
I was excited for new beginnings,
but also scared at the same time.

We pulled into the driveway
of our new town and new space.
Our next home looked different,
yet, I put a brave smile on my face.

We unpacked boxes and found places
for my belongings and cherished things.
It created a calming comfort,
even though it pulled at my heart strings.

I picked out a new outfit,
for my first day of school.
I wanted to fit in,
and for people to think I was cool.

Change was not that easy,
and some days were very hard,
But each day got better,
and I slowly let down my guard.

I started to feel more comfortable,
and our house slowly became a home.
I kept in touch with my old friends,
and made new ones of my own.

I learned it is ok for change,
and that is for certain.
Moving was not so bad,
and it made me a better person.

If you get the news that you are moving one day,
just know that YOU'VE GOT THIS
and you will find your way!

About the Author:

After graduating with a degree in Elementary Education, from Auburn University and a Master's Degree from the University of Montevallo, Leighton Harbuck began to foster her love for children and taught elementary school for many years. She then became a mother and stayed home with her babies. She loved every moment but had a constant feeling that she was meant for more. She decided to take after her mother and get her real estate license. Now, after many years in the real estate profession, Leighton is a top-producing agent in Birmingham, Alabama. Having a heart for children and real estate, she quickly realized the need for a book that would benefit children during the moving process. Leighton moved several times as a young child and knows firsthand the emotions brought on by having to leave family and friends. "From a House to a Home" helps children realize and deal with their emotions as they go through the moving process.

Leighton is married to Ryan Harbuck and together they have two beautiful girls, Mae and Maggie.